DOVER
CHILDREN'S THRIFT CLASSICS

A Little Princess

FRANCES HODGSON BURNETT

Adapted by Bob Blaisdell

Illustrated by Thea Kliros

DOVER PUBLICATIONS, INC.
Mineola, New York

DOVER CHILDREN'S THRIFT CLASSICS
EDITOR OF THIS VOLUME: CANDACE WARD

Copyright

Bibliographical Note

This Dover edition, first published in 1996, is a new abridgment, by Bob Blaisdell, of a standard edition of the work. The illustrations and introductory Note have been prepared specially for this edition.

Library of Congress Cataloging-in-Publication Data

Burnett, Frances Hodgson, 1849–1924.
    A little princess / Frances Hodgson Burnett ; adapted by Bob Blaisdell ; illustrated by Thea Kliros.
       p.   cm. — (Dover children's thrift classics)
    Summary: Sara Crewe, a pupil at Miss Minchin's London school, is left in poverty when her father dies but is later rescued by a mysterious benefactor.
    ISBN 0-486-29171-5 (pbk.)
    [1. Boarding schools—Fiction. 2. Schools—Fiction. 3. Orphans—Fiction. 4. London (England)—Fiction.] I. Blaisdell, Robert. II. Kliros, Thea, ill. III. Title. IV. Series.
PZ7.B934Lg 1996
[Fic]—dc20
                                  96-3150
                                     CIP
                                     AC

Manufactured in the United States of America
Dover Publications, Inc., 31 East 2nd Street, Mineola, N.Y. 11501

Note

In 1888, Frances Hodgson Burnett (1849–1924) published a short novel titled *Sara Crewe, or what happened at Miss Minchin's*. This work, which contained the basic story of *A Little Princess*, was adapted for the stage by Burnett in 1902. Three years later, Burnett published the present expanded version under the title *A Little Princess*.

Sara's story, now a classic of children's literature, is a riches to rags and back to riches tale. The pampered daughter of a wealthy Englishman, Sara is treated like a princess—until her father dies and leaves her in poverty. Her reversal of fortune, however, does not change Sara's good nature, and her vivid imagination allows her to pretend she is a princess on the inside even though she appears a beggar on the outside. Burnett provides a memorable cast of supporting characters, including the evil Miss Minchin, Becky the maid and Sara's dull-witted but kind friend Ermengarde. Young readers will share Sara's woes as well as her triumphs in this adaptation of Burnett's time-honored tale.

Contents

CHAPTER 1

Sara

ONCE ON A dark winter's day, when the fog hung thick in the streets of London, an odd-looking little girl sat in a cab with her father. She sat with her feet tucked under her, and leaned against her father, who held her in his arms, as she stared out of the window at the passing people.

Sara Crewe was only seven. At this moment she was remembering the voyage she had just made from Bombay with her father, Captain Crewe. What a strange thing it was that at one time one was in India in the blazing sun, and then in the middle of the ocean, and then driving through strange streets where the day was as dark as the night.

"Papa," she said, "is this the place?"

"Yes, little Sara, it is. We have reached it at last."

It seemed to her many years since he had begun to prepare her mind for "the place." Her mother had died when she was born, so she had never known or missed her. Her young, handsome, rich father seemed to be the only relation she had in the world. She had always lived in a beautiful bungalow, and had been used to seeing many servants who made salaams to her and called her "Missee Sahib."

During her short life only one thing had troubled her, and that thing was "the place" she was to be taken to some day. The climate of India was very bad for children, and as soon as possible they were sent away from it—generally to England and to school.

He held her in his arms as the cab rolled into the big, dull square in which stood the house that was their destination.

It was a big, dull, brick house, exactly like all the others in its row, but that on the front door there shone a brass plate on which was engraved:

MISS MINCHIN,
Select Seminary for Young Ladies.

"Here we are, Sara," said Captain Crewe. Then he lifted her out of the cab and they mounted the steps and rang the bell.

They were ushered into a drawing room, and there met Miss Minchin. She was tall and had large, cold, fishy eyes, and a large, cold, fishy smile.

"It will be a great privilege to have charge of such a beautiful and promising child, Captain Crewe," she said, taking Sara's hand and stroking it.

Sara stood quietly, with her eyes fixed upon Miss Minchin's face. "Why does she say I am a beautiful child?" she was thinking. "I am not beautiful at all. I have short black hair and green eyes; besides which, I am a thin child and not fair in the least. I am one of the ugliest children I ever saw. She is beginning by telling a story."

Sara was mistaken, however, in thinking she was an ugly child. She was a slim, supple creature, rather tall for her age, and had an attractive little face. Her hair was heavy and quite black and only curled at the tips; her eyes were greenish gray—big, wonderful eyes with long, black lashes.

She stood near her father and listened while he and Miss Minchin talked. She was to be what was known as "a parlor boarder." She was to have a pretty bedroom and sitting room of her own; she was to have a pony and carriage, and a maid to take the place of the ayah who had been her nurse in India.

"She is always sitting with her little nose burrowing into books," said Captain Crewe. "Drag her away from her books when she reads too much. Make her ride her pony or go out and buy a new doll. She ought to play more with dolls."

"Papa," said Sara, "dolls ought to be close friends. Emily is going to be my close friend."

"Who is Emily?" asked Miss Minchin.

"She is a doll I haven't got yet," said Sara. "She is a doll papa is going to buy for me. We are going out together to find her. She is going to be my friend when papa is gone."

Sara stayed with her father at his hotel until he sailed away again to India. They went out and visited many big shops together, and bought a great many things. They bought, indeed, a great many more things than Sara needed. The polite young women behind the shop counters whispered to each other that the odd little girl with the big eyes must be at least some foreign princess.

And at last they found Emily. As they were approaching a shop, Sara suddenly started and clutched her father's arm.

"Oh, papa!" she cried. "There is Emily!"

She was a large doll, but not too large to carry about easily; she had curling golden-brown hair, and her eyes were a deep, clear, gray-blue, with soft, thick eyelashes.

So Emily was bought.

Captain Crewe would really have enjoyed the shopping, but that a sad thought kept tugging at his heart. This all meant that he was going to be separated from his beloved little daughter.

The next day he took Sara to Miss Minchin's. He was to sail away the next morning. He would write to Sara twice a week, and she was to be given every pleasure she asked for. Then he went with her into her little sitting room and they bade each other good-by.

When the cab drove away from the door, Sara was sitting on the floor of her sitting room, with her hands under her chin and her eyes following it until it had turned the corner of the square. Emily was sitting by her, and she looked after it, too.

When Sara entered the schoolroom the next morning everybody looked at her. They knew that she was Miss Minchin's show pupil and was considered a credit to the establishment.

Sara sat down quietly in her seat; she had been placed near Miss Minchin's desk. She looked back quietly at the children who looked at her. After she had sat for a few minutes, Miss Minchin rapped upon her desk.

"Young ladies," she said, "I wish to introduce you to your new companion." All the little girls rose in their places, and Sara rose also. "I shall expect you all to be very agreeable to Miss Crewe; she has just come to us from a great distance—in fact, from India.

As soon as lessons are over you must make each other's acquaintance."

The pupils bowed, and Sara made a little curtsy, and they sat down and looked at each other again.

"Sara," said Miss Minchin, "come here to me. As your papa has hired a French maid for you, I conclude that he wishes you to make a special study of the French language."

"I think he hired her," said Sara, "because he thought I would like her, Miss Minchin."

"I am afraid," said Miss Minchin, "that you have been a very spoiled little girl and always imagine that things are done because you like them. My impression is that your papa wished you to learn French."

The truth was that Sara could not remember the time when she had not seemed to know French. Her father had often spoken it to her when she had been a baby. Her mother had been a French woman, and Captain Crewe had loved her language, so it happened that Sara had always heard and been familiar with it.

"I—I have never really learned French, but—but—" she began.

"That is enough," said Miss Minchin. "If you have not learned, you must begin at once. The French master, Monsieur Dufarge, will be here in a few minutes."

He arrived very shortly afterward. He was a nice, middle-aged Frenchman. "Is this a new pupil for me, madame?" he said to Miss Minchin.

"She does not seem to wish to learn," said Miss Minchin.

"Perhaps when we begin to study together," said Monsieur Dufarge, "I may show you that it is a charming language."

Little Sara rose in her seat. She began to explain quite simply in pretty and fluent French that Madame had not understood. She had not learned French exactly—not out of books—but her papa and other people had always spoken it to her, and she had read it and written it as she had read and written English.

"Ah, madame," said Monsieur Dufarge to Miss Minchin, "there is not much I can teach her. She has not *learned* French; she *is* French. Her accent is exquisite."

"You ought to have told me," exclaimed Miss Minchin, turning to Sara.

"I—I tried," said Sara. "I—I suppose I did not begin right."

Miss Minchin knew Sara had tried, and that it had not been her fault that she was not allowed to explain. But when she saw that Lavinia and Jessie were giggling behind their French books, she felt angry.

"Silence, young ladies!" she said, rapping upon the desk. "Silence at once!"

And she began from that minute to feel rather a grudge against her show pupil.

As Sara sat at Miss Minchin's side, aware that the

whole schoolroom was observing her, she noticed one little girl, about her own age, who looked at her very hard with a pair of dull blue eyes. She was a plump child who had a good-natured, pouting mouth. Her blond hair was braided in a pigtail, tied with a ribbon.

Sara took a fancy to the plump little girl, and kept glancing toward her through the morning. When lessons were over and the pupils gathered together in groups to talk, Sara looked for the girl, and finding her bundled rather sadly in a window-seat, she walked over to her.

"What is your name?" asked Sara.

"My name's Ermengarde St. John."

"Mine is Sara Crewe. Yours is very pretty. It sounds like a story book."

"Do you like it?" said Ermengarde. "I—I like yours."

Miss St. John's chief trouble in life was that she learned things and forgot them; or, if she remembered them, she did not understand them. So it was natural that, having met Sara, she should sit and stare at her with admiration.

"You can speak French, can't you?"

"I can speak it because I have heard it all my life," Sara answered. "You could speak it if you had always heard it."

"Oh, no, I couldn't," said Ermengarde. "I never could speak it!— You are *clever*, aren't you?"

"Would you like to see Emily?" asked Sara, changing the subject.

"Who is Emily?"

"Come up to my room and see," said Sara, holding out her hand.

Emily was the most beautiful doll Ermengarde had ever seen.

"This is Ermengarde St. John, Emily. Ermengarde, this is Emily. Would you like to hold her?"

"Oh, may I?" said Ermengarde.

Never in her dull, short life had Miss St. John dreamed of such an hour as the one she spent with the odd new pupil.

Sara sat upon the hearth-rug and told her strange things. She sat rather huddled up, and her green eyes shone and her cheeks flushed. She told stories of the voyage, and stories of India; but what fascinated Ermengarde was her fancy about the dolls who walked and talked, and who could do anything they chose when the human beings were out of the room, but who must keep their powers a secret and so flew back to their places "like lightning" when people turned to the room.

"We couldn't do it," said Sara. "You see, it's magic."

After the stories, Ermengarde said, "Lavinia and Jessie are best friends. I wish we could be best friends. Would you have me for yours? You're clever, and I'm the stupidest child in the school, but I—oh, I do so like you!"

"I'm glad of that," said Sara. "Yes. We will be friends. And I'll tell you what, I can help you with your French lessons. Things happen to people by accident. A lot of nice accidents have happened to me. It just *happened* that I always liked lessons and books, and could remember things when I learned them. It just happened that I was born with a father who was beautiful and nice and clever, and could give me everything I liked. Perhaps I have not really a good temper at all, but if you have everything you want and everyone is kind to you, how can you help but be good-tempered? I don't know how I shall ever find out whether I am really a nice child or a horrid one. Perhaps I'm a hideous child, and no one will ever know, just because I never have any trials."

CHAPTER 2

Becky

Sara was a friendly little soul, and shared her privileges and belongings with a free hand. The little ones, who were used to being ordered out of the way by mature ladies aged ten and twelve, were never made to cry by this most envied of them all. She was a motherly young person, and when people fell down and scraped their knees, she ran and helped them up and patted them, or found in her pocket a bonbon or some other article of a soothing nature. She never pushed them out of her way or alluded to their years as a humiliation.

So the younger children adored Sara. More than once she had been known to have a tea party, made up of these despised ones, in her own room. And Emily had been played with, and Emily's own tea service used—the one with cups which held quite a lot of much-sweetened weak tea and had blue flowers on them. From that afternoon Sara was regarded as a goddess and a queen by the entire alphabet class.

When she sat or stood in the midst of a circle and began to invent wonderful things, her green eyes grew big and shining, her cheeks flushed, and, with-

13

out knowing that she was doing it, she began to act and made what she told lovely or alarming by the raising or dropping of her voice, the bend and sway of her slim body, and the dramatic movement of her hands. She forgot that she was talking to listening children; she saw and lived with the fairy folk, or the kings and queens and beautiful ladies, whose adventures she was narrating.

She had been at Miss Minchin's school about two years when, one foggy winter's afternoon, as she was getting out of her carriage, wrapped up in her velvets and furs, she caught sight of a little figure standing on the steps, and stretching its neck so that its wide-open eyes might peer at her through the railings. When Sara looked at the smudgy face she smiled, because it was her way to smile at people.

But the owner of the smudgy face evidently was afraid; she dodged out of sight like a Jack-in-the-box and scurried back into the kitchen. That very evening, as Sara was sitting in the midst of a group of listeners in a corner of the schoolroom telling one of her stories, the very same figure timidly entered the room, carrying a coal box much too heavy for her, and knelt down upon the hearth rug to replenish the fire and sweep up the ashes.

She was cleaner than when she peeped through the railings, but she looked just as frightened. She put on pieces of coal with her fingers so that she might make no disturbing noise, and she swept about the fire irons very softly. But Sara saw in two minutes that

she was interested in what was going on, and that she was doing her work slowly in the hope of catching a word here and there. And realizing this, she raised her voice.

"The Mermaids swam softly about in the crystal-green water, and dragged after them a fishing-net woven of deep-sea pearls," she said. "The Princess sat on the white rock and watched them."

It was a story about a princess who was loved by a Prince Merman, and went to live with him in shining caves under the sea.

The sound of the story so lured the girl that she actually sat down upon her heels as she knelt on the hearth rug, and the brush hung in her fingers. The voice of the storyteller went on and drew her with it into winding grottos under the sea.

The hearth brush fell from her hand, and Lavinia looked round.

"That girl has been listening," she said.

The culprit snatched up her brush, and scrambled to her feet. She caught at the coal box and hurried out of the room.

"I knew she was listening," said Sara. "Why shouldn't she?"

"Well," said Lavinia, "I do not know whether your mamma would like you to tell stories to servant girls, but I know *my* mamma wouldn't like *me* to do it."

"My mamma!" said Sara. "I don't believe she would mind in the least. She knows that stories belong to everybody."

"I thought," answered Lavinia, "that your mamma was dead. How can she know things?"

"Do you think she *doesn't* know things?" said Sara, in her stern little voice.

And she marched out of the room, rather hoping that she might see the little servant again somewhere, but she found no trace of her.

"Who is that little girl who makes the fires?" she asked Mariette that night.

Ah, indeed, Mademoiselle Sara might well ask. She was a sad little thing who had just taken the place of scullery maid—and she was everything else besides. She blacked boots and grates, and carried heavy coal-scuttles up and down stairs, and scrubbed floors and cleaned windows, and was ordered about by every-body. She was fourteen years old, but she was so stunted in growth that she looked about twelve.

"What is her name?" asked Sara.

Her name was Becky. Mariette heard everyone below-stairs calling, "Becky, do this," and "Becky, do that," every five minutes in the day.

Sara sat and looked into the fire, reflecting on Becky for some time. She thought Becky looked as if she never had quite enough to eat. Her very eyes were hungry. She hoped she should see her again.

A few weeks later, on another foggy afternoon, when she entered her sitting room she found herself confronting a rather pathetic picture. In her own special easy-chair before the bright fire, Becky—with a coal smudge on her nose and several on her apron, with her poor little cap hanging half off her head, and an empty coal box on the floor near her—sat fast asleep, tired out. She had been sent up to put the bedrooms in order for the evening. There were a great many of them, and she had been running about all day. Sara's rooms she had saved until the last. She saved it until the end of her afternoon's work, because she always hoped to snatch a few minutes to sit down in the soft chair and look about her, and think about the wonderful good fortune of the child who owned such surroundings and who went out on cold days in beautiful hats and coats.

On this afternoon, when she had sat down, the sensation of relief to her short, aching legs had been so delightful that it had seemed to soothe her whole body, and she fell fast asleep.

Sara had been taking her dancing lesson, and when she entered the room, she floated in with a few butterfly steps—and there sat Becky, nodding her cap sideways off her head.

"Oh," cried Sara, when she saw her. "That poor thing!" She crept toward her quietly, and stood looking at her. Becky gave a little snore.

After a few minutes Becky started, and opened her eyes with a frightened gasp. She did not know she had fallen asleep. She had only sat down for one moment—and here she found herself staring at the wonderful pupil.

She sprang up and clutched at her cap. She felt it dangling over her ear. To have fallen asleep on such a young lady's chair! She would be turned out of doors without pay.

"Oh, miss! Oh, miss!" she stuttered. "I arst yer pardon, miss! Oh, I do, miss!"

"Don't be frightened," Sara said. "It doesn't matter the least bit."

"I didn't go to do it, miss," protested Becky. "It was the warm fire—an' me bein' so tired. It—it *wasn't* impertinence!"

Sara broke into a friendly laugh, and put her hand on her shoulder.

"You were tired," she said; "you could not help it. You are not really awake yet."

How poor Becky stared at her! Becky had never heard such a nice, friendly sound in anyone's voice before. She was used to being ordered about and scolded, and having her ears boxed. And this one was looking at her as if she were not a culprit at all— as if she had a right to be tired—even to fall asleep!

"Ain't—ain't yer angry, miss?" she gasped. "Ain't yer goin' to tell the missus?"

"No," cried out Sara. "Of course I'm not."

The woeful fright in the coal-smudged face made her suddenly so sorry that she could scarcely bear it. She put her hand against Becky's cheek.

"Why," she said, "we are just the same—I am only a little girl like you. It's just an accident that I am not you, and you are not me!"

Becky did not understand in the least.

"A' accident, miss?"

"Yes," Sara answered. But she realized Becky did not know what she meant. "Have you done your work? Dare you stay here a few minutes?"

"Here, miss? Me?"

Sara ran to the door, opened it, and looked out and listened.

"No one is anywhere about," she explained. "If your bedrooms are finished, perhaps you might stay a tiny while. I thought—perhaps—you might like a piece of cake."

The next ten minutes seemed to Becky like a sort of crazy dream. Sara opened a cupboard, and gave her a thick slice of cake. She seemed to rejoice when it was devoured in hungry bites. She talked and asked questions. Becky once or twice gathered boldness enough to ask a question or so herself.

"Is that—" she asked, looking at the rose-colored frock Sara had on, "is that there your best?"

"It is one of my dancing frocks," answered Sara. "I like it, don't you?"

Becky said, "Onct I see a princess. I was standin' in the street with the crowd outside Covin' Garden, watchin' the swells go inter the operer. An' there

was one everyone stared at most. They ses to each other, 'That's the princess.' She was a growed-up young lady, but she was pink all over—gownd an' cloak, an' flowers an' all. I called her to mind the minnit I see you, sittin' there on the table, miss. You looked like her."

"I've often thought," said Sara, "that I should like to be a princess; I wonder what it feels like. I believe I will begin pretending I am one."

Becky did not understand her in the least. She watched her with a sort of adoration.

"Becky," said Sara, "would you like to hear the rest of the story I was telling a few weeks ago?"

"Me hear it?" she cried. "Like as if I was a pupil, miss! All about the Prince—and the little white Mer-babies swimming about laughing—with stars in their hair?"

Sara nodded. "You haven't time to hear it now, I'm afraid, but if you will tell me just what time you come to do my rooms, I will try to be here and tell you a bit of it every day until it is finished. It's a lovely long one—and I'm always putting new bits to it."

"Then," said Becky, "I wouldn't mind *how* heavy the coal boxes was—or *what* the cook done to me, if—if I might have that to think of."

"You may," said Sara. "I'll tell it *all* to you."

When Becky went downstairs, she was not the same Becky who had staggered up, loaded down by the weight of the coal scuttle. She had an extra piece of cake in her pocket, and she had been fed and warmed, but not only by cake and fire. Something else had warmed and fed her, and the something else was Sara.

CHAPTER 3

The Diamond Mines

NOT VERY LONG after this a very exciting thing happened. Not only Sara, but the entire school, found it exciting. In one of his letters Captain Crewe told a most interesting story. A friend had unexpectedly come to see him in India. He was the owner of a large piece of land upon which diamonds had been found, and he was developing the mines. If all went as was expected, he would become possessed of such wealth as it made one dizzy to think of; and because he was fond of the friend of his school days, he had given him an opportunity to share in this fortune by becoming a partner in his scheme.

After this, the girls who were jealous of Sara used to speak of her as "Princess Sara" whenever they wished to be disdainful, and those who were fond of her gave her the name among themselves as a term of affection.

A few weeks before Sara's eleventh birthday a letter came to her from her father. He was not very well, and was evidently overweighted by the business connected with the diamond mines.

"You see, little Sara," he wrote, "your daddy is not a businessman at all, and figures and documents bother him. He does not really understand them, and all this seems so enormous. If my little missus were here, I dare say she would give me some good advice. You would, wouldn't you, Little Missus?"

He had made wonderful preparations for her birthday. Among other things, a new doll had been ordered in Paris. When Sara had replied to the letter asking her if the doll would be an acceptable present, Sara wrote:

"I am getting very old. You see, I shall never live to have another doll given me. This will be my last doll. No one could ever take Emily's place, but I should respect the Last Doll very much; and I am sure the school would love it."

Captain Crewe had a splitting headache when he read this letter in his bungalow in India. The table

before him was heaped with papers and letters which were alarming him and filling him with anxious dread, but he laughed as he had not laughed for weeks.

"Oh," he said, "she's better fun every year she lives. God grant this business may right itself and leave me free to run home and see her."

The birthday was to be celebrated by great festivities. The boxes containing the presents were to be opened with great ceremony, and there was to be a glittering feast spread in Miss Minchin's room. When the day arrived the whole house was in a whirl of excitement.

When Sara went into her sitting room in the morning, she found on the table a small, dumpy package, tied up in a piece of brown paper. She knew it was a present, and she opened it. It was a square pincushion, and black pins had been stuck carefully into it to form the words, "Menny hapy returns."

"Oh!" cried Sara, "what pains she has taken! I like it so, it—it makes me feel sorrowful."

And just at that very moment, she heard the door being pushed open and saw Becky peeping round it.

There was a grin on her face, and she shuffled forward and stood pulling at her fingers.

"Do yer like it, Miss Sara?" she said. "Do yer?"

"Like it?" cried Sara. "You darling Becky, you made it all yourself."

Becky gave a joyful sniff, and her eyes looked quite moist with delight.

"It ain't nothin' but flannin, an' the flannin ain't
new; but I wanted to give yer somethin' an' I made it
of nights. I knew yer could *pretend* it was satin with
diamond pins in. *I* tried to when I was makin' it."

Sara flew at her and hugged her.

"Oh, Becky!" she cried out with a laugh. "I love
you, Becky—I do, I do!"

"Oh, miss!" breathed Becky. "Thank yer, miss, kind-
ly; it ain't good enough for that. The—the flannin
wasn't new."

When Sara entered the holly-hung schoolroom in the afternoon, she was led grandly in and felt shy when the big girls stared at her and the little ones began to squirm joyously in their seats.

Miss Minchin announced to the servants, including poor Becky, who had helped carry in Sara's boxed presents, "You may leave us."

"If you please, Miss Minchin," said Sara, "mayn't Becky stay?"

"Becky!" exclaimed Miss Minchin. "My dearest Sara!"

"I want her because I know she will like to see the presents," said Sara. "She is a little girl, too. And I know she would enjoy herself. Please let her stay— because it is my birthday."

"As you ask it as a birthday favor—she may stay." Miss Minchin cleared her throat and spoke again: "Now, young ladies, I have a few words to say to you. Sara has become my most accomplished pupil. Her French and her dancing are a credit to the seminary. Her manners—which have caused you to call her Princess Sara—are perfect. Her amiability she exhibits by giving you this afternoon's party. I hope you appreciate her generosity. I wish you to express your appreciation of it by saying all aloud together, 'Thank you, Sara!' "

The entire schoolroom rose to its feet and said, "Thank you, Sara!"

She made a curtsy. "Thank you," she said, "for coming to my party."

"Very pretty, indeed, Sara," said Miss Minchin. "That is what a real princess does when the populace applauds her. Now I will leave you to enjoy yourselves."

The instant Miss Minchin had swept out of the room, the girls tumbled out of their seats. There was a rush toward the boxes.

When Sara took out the Last Doll it was so magnificent that the children uttered delighted groans of joy.

"She is almost as big as Lottie," someone gasped.

Never had the schoolroom been in such an uproar. For the doll there were lace collars and silk stockings and handkerchiefs; there was a jewel case containing a necklace and a tiara; there were ball dresses and there were hats and fans.

"Suppose," Sara said, as she stood by the table, "suppose the doll understands human talk and feels proud of being admired."

"You are always supposing things," said Lavinia, who did not like Sara. "It's all very well to suppose things if you have everything. Could you suppose and pretend if you were a beggar and lived in a dusty attic?"

"I *believe* I could," she said. "If one was a beggar, one would have to suppose and pretend all the time. But it mightn't be easy."

She often thought afterward how strange it was that just as she had finished saying this, Miss Amelia, Miss Minchin's sister, came into the room.

"Sara," she said, "your papa's solicitor, Mr. Barrow, has called to see Miss Minchin, and, as she must talk to him alone and the refreshments are laid in her parlor, you had all better come and have your feast now, so that my sister can have her interview here in the schoolroom."

She led the girls away, leaving the Last Doll sitting upon a chair with her wardrobe scattered about her.

Miss Minchin came into the room accompanied by a little gentleman, who looked rather disturbed.

"Pray be seated, Mr. Barrow," she said.

"He spent money lavishly enough, that young man. Birthday presents to a child eleven years old! The late Mr. Crewe—"

"The *late* Captain Crewe," Miss Minchin cried out. "The *late*! You don't come to tell me that Captain Crewe is—"

"He's dead, ma'am," said Mr. Barrow. "Died of jungle fever and business troubles combined."

"What *were* his business troubles?" she said.

"Diamond mines," answered Mr. Barrow, "and dear friends—and ruin."

"Ruin!"

"Lost every penny. That young man had too much money. The dear friend was mad on the subject of the diamond mine. He put all his own money into it, and all Captain Crewe's. Then the dear friend ran away. The shock was too much for Captain Crewe. He died delirious, raving about his little girl—and didn't leave a penny."

Now Miss Minchin understood, and never had she

received such a blow in her life. Her show pupil, her show patron, swept away from the Select Seminary at one blow.

"Do you mean to tell me," she cried out, "that he left *nothing!* That the child is a beggar! That she is left on my hands a little pauper instead of an heiress?"

"She is certainly left a beggar," he replied. "And she is certainly left on your hands, ma'am—as she hasn't a relation in the world that we know of."

"But what am I to do?"

"There isn't anything to do. Captain Crewe is dead. The child is left a pauper. Nobody is responsible for her but you."

"I have been robbed and cheated," said Miss Minchin. "I will turn her out into the street!"

"I wouldn't do that, madam," said Mr. Barrow. "It wouldn't look well. You had better keep her and make use of her."

After he left, Miss Minchin ordered her sister to go at once and stop the party and tell Sara her father had died.

Miss Amelia did as she was told and then returned. "Sister," she said, "Sara is the strangest child I ever saw. She actually made no fuss at all. When I told her what had happened, she just stood quite still and looked at me without making a sound. Her eyes seemed to get bigger and bigger, and she went quite pale. When I had finished, she still stood staring for a few seconds, and then her chin began to shake, and she turned round and ran out of the room and upstairs."

CHAPTER 4
In the Attic

WHEN SARA CAME a few hours later into Miss Minchin's sitting room in answer to her call, her face was white and her eyes had dark rings around them. Her mouth was set as if she did not wish to reveal what she had suffered and was suffering. She had put on a cast-aside black-velvet frock. It was too short and tight, and her slender legs looked long and thin, showing themselves from beneath the short skirt. As she had not found a piece of black ribbon, her short, thick, black hair tumbled loosely about her face. She held Emily tightly in one arm, and Emily was swathed in a piece of black material.

"Put down your doll," said Miss Minchin. "What do you mean by bringing her here?"

"No," Sara answered. "I will not put her down. She is all I have. My papa gave her to me."

"You will have no time for dolls in future," said Miss Minchin. "You will have to work and make yourself useful. I suppose Miss Amelia has explained matters to you."

"Yes," answered Sara. "My papa is dead. He left me no money. I am quite poor."

"You are a beggar," said Miss Minchin. "You have no one to do anything for you, unless I choose to keep you here out of charity. You are not a princess any longer. Your carriage and your pony will be sent away—your maid will be dismissed. You will wear your oldest and plainest clothes—your extravagant ones are no longer suited to your station. You are like Becky—you must work for your living."

"Can I work?" said Sara. "If I can work it will not matter so much. What can I do?"

"You can do anything you are told," was the answer. "You are a sharp child, and pick up things readily. If you make yourself useful I may let you stay here. You speak French well, and you can help with the younger children. You will also run errands and help in the kitchen as well as in the schoolroom. If you don't please me, you will be sent away. Remember that. Now go."

Sara wished to go to her room and lie down on the tiger-skin, and look into the fire and think and think and think. But just before she reached the landing Miss Amelia came out of the door and closed it behind her, and stood before it."

"You—you are not to go in there," she said. "That is not your room now."

All at once, Sara understood. This was the beginning of the change Miss Minchin had spoken of.

"Where is my room?" she asked.

"You are to sleep in the attic next to Becky."

Sara knew where it was. She turned and mounted up two flights of stairs. She felt as if she were walking away and leaving far behind her the world in which the other child, who no longer seemed herself, had lived. This child, in her short, tight old frock, climbing the stairs to the attic, was quite a different creature.

When she reached the attic door and opened it, her heart gave a thump. Then she shut the door and stood against it and looked about her.

Yes, this was another world. The room had a slanting roof and was whitewashed. The whitewash was dingy and had fallen off in places. There was a rusty grate, an old iron bedstead, and a hard bed covered with a faded coverlet. Some pieces of furniture too much worn to be used downstairs had been sent up. Under the skylight in the roof, which showed nothing but a small piece of sky, there stood a red footstool. Sara went to it and sat down. She seldom cried. She did not cry now. She laid Emily across her knees and put her face down upon her and her arms around her, and sat there, her little black head resting

on the black draperies, not saying one word, not making one sound.

And as she sat in this silence there came a low tap at the door—such a low one that she did not at first hear it, and, indeed, was not roused until the door was pushed open and a poor tear-smeared face appeared peeping round it. It was Becky.

"Oh, miss," she said. "Might I—would you allow me—jest to come in?"

Sara lifted her head and looked at her. She tried to begin a smile, and somehow she could not. Suddenly, she held out her hand and gave a little sob.

"Oh, Becky," she said. "I told you we were just the same—only two little girls—just two little girls. You see how true it is. There's no difference now. I'm not a princess anymore."

Becky ran to her and caught her hand, and hugged it to her chest, kneeling beside her and sobbing with love and pain.

"Yes, miss, you are," she cried. "Whats'ever 'appens to you—whats'ever—you'd be a princess all the same—an' nothin' couldn't make you nothin' different."

* * *

The first night she spent in her attic was a thing Sara never forgot. "My papa is dead!" she kept whispering to herself. "My papa is dead!"

The wind howled over the roof among the chimneys. Then there were scratchings and squeakings in the walls. She knew what they meant. They meant rats and mice who were either fighting with each other or playing together. Once or twice she even heard sharp-toed feet scurrying across the floor, and she started up in bed and sat trembling. When she lay down again she covered her head with her bedclothes.

The change in her life did not come about gradually, but was made all at once.

When she went down to breakfast she saw that her seat at Miss Minchin's side was occupied by Lavinia.

Miss Minchin spoke to her coldly, saying, "You will begin your new duties, Sara, by taking your seat with the younger children at a smaller table. You must keep them quiet."

That was the beginning, and from day to day the duties given to her were added to. She taught the younger children French and heard their other lessons, and these were the least of her labors. It was found that she could be made use of in numberless directions. She could be sent on errands at any time and in all weathers. The cook and housemaids took their tone from Miss Minchin, and rather enjoyed ordering about the "young one" who had been made so much fuss over for so long.

If she had been older, Miss Minchin would have given her the bigger girls to teach and saved money by dismissing an instructress; but while she remained and looked like a child, she could be made more useful as a sort of little errand girl and maid of all work.

Her own lessons became a thing of the past. She was taught nothing, and only after long and busy days spent in running here and there at everybody's orders was she grudgingly allowed to go into the deserted schoolroom, with a pile of old books, and study alone at night.

One of the most curious things in her new existence was her changed position among the pupils. Instead of being a sort of small royal personage among them, she no longer seemed to be one of their number at all. She was kept so constantly at work that she scarcely ever had an opportunity of speaking to any of them.

"I will not have her forming intimacies and talking to the other children," declared Miss Minchin of Sara. "Girls like to complain, and if she begins to tell stories about herself, she will become an ill-used heroine. It is better that she should live a separate life—one suited to her circumstances. I am giving her a home, and that is more than she has any right to expect from me."

Sara did not expect much, and was far too proud to try to continue to be intimate with girls who evidently felt as if, when they spoke to her, they were addressing a servant.

As she became shabbier and more forlorn-looking, she was told that she had better take her meals downstairs.

"Solidiers don't complain," she would say between her teeth, "and I am not going to. I will pretend this is part of a war."

But there were times when her heart might almost have broken but for two people.

The first was Becky. Throughout all the first night spent in the attic, she had felt a comfort in knowing that on the other side of the wall in which rats scuffled and squeaked there was another young human creature. They had little chance to speak to each other during the day.

But before daybreak Becky used to slip into Sara's attic and button her dress and give her such help as she needed before she went downstairs to light the kitchen fire. And when night came Sara always heard the knock at her door which meant that her handmaid was ready to help her again if she was needed.

The second comforter was Ermengarde. One night, when Sara went to her attic, she was surprised to see a glimmer of light coming from under the attic door.

Sara opened the door and cried, "Ermengarde! You will get into trouble."

Ermengarde stumbled up from her footstool. She shuffled across the attic in her bedroom slippers, which were too large for her. Her eyes and nose were pink from crying.

"I know I shall—if I'm found out," she said. "But I don't care a bit. I couldn't bear it any more. Sara, do you think you can bear living here?"

"If I pretend it's quite different, I can," she answered. "Or if I pretend it is a place in a story. Other people have lived in worse places. Think of the people in the Bastille! Yes, that will be a good place to pretend about. I am a prisoner in the Bastille. I have been here for years and years—and everybody has forgotten about me. Miss Minchin is the jailer—and Becky is the prisoner in the next cell. I shall pretend that, and it will be a great comfort."

Ermengarde exclaimed, "And will you tell me all about it? May I creep up here at night, whenever it is safe, and hear the things you have made up in the day? It will seem as if we were more best friends than ever."

"Yes," answered Sara, nodding. "Adversity tries people, and mine has tried you and proved how nice you are."

CHAPTER 5

Melchisedec

AFTER ERMENGARDE had gone downstairs again, Sara stood in the middle of the attic and looked about her. The bed was hard and covered with a faded quilt. The whitewashed wall showed its broken patches, the floor was cold and bare, the grate was broken and rusty. She sat down on the battered footstool and let her head drop in her hands.

"It's a lonely place," she said. "Sometimes it's the loneliest place in the world."

She was sitting in this way when her attention was attracted by a sound near her. A large rat was sitting up on his hind quarters and sniffing the air. He looked at Sara with his bright eyes, as if he were asking a question.

"I dare say it's rather hard to be a rat," mused Sara. "Nobody likes you. People jump and run away and scream out, 'Oh, a horrid rat!' I shouldn't like people to scream and jump and say, 'Oh, a horrid Sara!' the moment they saw me."

She had sat so quietly that the rat had begun to take courage. He was very hungry. He had a wife and a large family in the wall, and he felt he would risk a good deal for a few crumbs.

"Come on," said Sara. "I'm not a trap. You can have the crumbs, poor thing! Prisoners in the Bastille used to make friends with rats. Suppose I make friends with you."

He went softly toward the crumbs and began to eat them.

She sat and watched him without making any movement. He took a last big crumb for his children and then fled back to the wall, slipped down a crack, and was gone.

"I do believe I could make friends with him," said Sara.

Visits from Ermengarde were rare, and Sara lived a strange and lonely life. It was a lonelier life when she was downstairs than when she was in her attic. She had no one to talk to; and when she was sent out on errands and walked through the streets, she felt as if the crowds hurrying past her made her loneliness greater.

In the evening, when she passed houses whose windows were lighted up, she used to look into the warm rooms and amuse herself by imagining things about the people she saw sitting before the fires or about the tables. There were several families in the square in which Miss Minchin lived. The one she liked best she called the Large Family. She called it the Large Family not because the members of it were big—for, indeed, most of them were little—but because there were so many of them. There were eight children in the Large Family, and a stout, rosy mother, and a stout, rosy father, and a stout, rosy grandmother, and any number of servants.

One evening a very funny thing happened. Several of the family were evidently going to a children's party, and just as Sara was about to pass the door they were crossing the pavement to get into the carriage which was waiting for them. Sara paused to look at one of the young boys, following two of his

sisters. He was five. It was Christmas time, and the Large Family had been hearing many stories about children who were poor and had no mammas and papas to fill their stockings—children who were cold and thinly clad and hungry. The boy had a desire to find such a poor child and give her a certain sixpence he possessed. He saw Sara standing on the wet pavement in her shabby frock and hat, with her old basket on her arm.

He thought that her eyes looked hungry. She had big eyes and a thin face and thin legs and a common basket and poor clothes. So he put his hand in his pocket and found his sixpence and walked up to her.

"Here, poor little girl," he said. "Here is a sixpence. I will give it to you."

Sara all at once realized that she looked exactly like poor children she had seen, in her better days.

"Oh, no!" she said. "Oh, no, thank you. I mustn't take it, indeed!"

But the boy thrust the sixpence into her hand.

"Yes, you must take it, poor little girl!" he insisted. "You can buy things to eat with it. It is a whole sixpence!"

He looked so likely to be disappointed if she did not take it, that Sara knew she must not refuse him.

"Thank you," she said. "You are a kind, kind little darling thing." And as he scrambled joyfully into the carriage she went away. She had known that she looked odd and shabby, but until now she had not known that she might be taken for a beggar.

Sara managed to bore a hole in the sixpence and hung it on an old bit of narrow ribbon round her neck. Her affection for the Large Family increased— as, indeed, her affection for everything she could love increased. She grew fonder and fonder of Becky, and she used to look forward to the two mornings a week when she went into the schoolroom to give the little ones their French lesson.

With Melchisedec, the name she had given the rat in her attic, she had become so friendly that he actually brought Mrs. Melchisedec with him some- times, and now and then brought one or two of his children.

She wished that someone would take the empty house next door. She wished it because of the attic

window which was so near hers. It seemed as if it
would be so nice to see it propped open someday
and a head and shoulders rising out of the square
opening.

One morning, on turning the corner of the square
after a visit to the grocer's, the butcher's, and the
baker's, she saw, to her great delight, that during her
long set of errands, a van full of furniture had stopped
before the next house, the front doors were thrown
open, and men were going in and out carrying heavy
packages and pieces of furniture.

"All the things look rather grand. I suppose it is a
rich family," she thought.

At night, after her work was done, Becky came in to
see her fellow prisoner and bring her news.

"It's a' Nindian gentleman that's coming to live
next door, miss," she said. "He's very rich, an' he's ill,
an' the gentleman of the Large Family is his lawyer.
He's had a lot of trouble, an' it's made him ill an' low
in his mind."

He was a single man with no family at all.

CHAPTER 6

The Indian Gentleman

ONE EVENING, a few days after the sickly Indian gentleman was brought to his new home, Sara found it easier than usual to slip away and go upstairs.

She mounted her table and stood looking out at the fine sunset. There were floods of molten gold covering the west. The birds flying across the tops of the houses showed quite black against the yellow light.

She suddenly turned her head because she heard a sound a few yards away from her. A strange squeaky chattering came from the window of the next attic. Someone had come to look at the sunset as she had. There was the white-swathed form and dark-faced, white-turbaned head of a Lascar, a native Indian man-servant, emerging from the skylight, and the sound she had heard came from a small monkey he held in his arms.

As Sara looked toward him he looked toward her. She smiled at him.

He smiled back. At the same time he loosened his hold on the monkey, which suddenly broke free, jumped on to the slates, ran across them chattering, and actually leaped onto Sara's shoulder, and from

47

there down into her attic room. It made her laugh and delighted her; but she knew he must be restored to his master, and she wondered how this was to be done.

She spoke to the Indian man-servant, "Will he let me catch him?"

The young man, whose name was Ram Dass, explained that he was a servant of the gentleman downstairs. The monkey was a good monkey and would not bite; but, unfortunately, he was difficult to catch. If Missee Sahib would permit Ram Dass, he himself could cross the roof to her room, enter the windows, and regain the little animal.

"Can you get across?" asked Sara.

"In a moment," he answered.

"Then come," she said. "He is flying from side to side of the room as if he was frightened."

Ram Dass slipped through his attic window and crossed to hers as steadily and lightly as if he had walked on roofs all his life. He slipped through the skylight and dropped upon his feet without a sound. Then he turned to Sara and salaamed again. The monkey saw him and uttered a little scream. In a few moments, however, the monkey sprang chattering on to Ram Dass's shoulder and sat there clinging to his neck.

Ram Dass thanked Sara profoundly. She had seen that he had taken in at a glance all the bare shabbiness of the room, but he spoke to her as if he were speaking to the little daughter of a rajah. He did not presume to remain more than a few moments. This little evil one, he said, stroking the monkey, was, in truth, not so evil as he seemed, and his master, who was ill, was sometimes amused by him. He would have been made sad if his favorite had run away and been lost. Then he salaamed once more and got through the skylight and across the slates again.

When he had gone Sara remembered that she—the drudge whom the cook had said insulting things to an hour ago—had only a few years ago been surrounded by people who all treated her as Ram Dass had treated her. It was like a sort of dream. It certainly seemed that there was no way in which any change could take place. She knew what Miss Minchin intended that her future should be. Then a thought came back to her which made the color rise in her cheek and a spark light itself in her eyes.

"Whatever comes," she said, "cannot alter one thing. If I am a princess in rags and tatters, I can be a princess inside. It would be easy to be a princess if I were dressed in cloth of gold, but it is a great deal more of a triumph to be one all the time when no one knows it."

In the kitchen there was much discussion of the Indian gentleman next door. He was not an Indian gentleman really, but an Englishman who had lived in India. He had met with great misfortunes which had for a time so imperilled his whole fortune that he had thought himself ruined. The shock had been so great that he had almost died of brain fever; and ever since he had been shattered in health, though his fortunes had changed and all his possessions had been restored to him.

"He felt as my papa felt," thought Sara. "He was ill as my papa was; but he did not die."

So her heart was drawn to him. When she was sent out at night she used to feel quite glad, because there was always a chance that the curtains of the house next door might not yet be closed and she could look into the warm room and see her adopted friend.

The Indian gentleman's name was Mr. Carrisford. He was very much interested when he heard from Ram Dass of the adventure of the monkey on the roof. Ram Dass made for him a very clear picture of the attic and its bare floor and broken plaster, the rusty, empty grate, and the hard, narrow bed.

And hearing of this girl made Mr. Carrisford think of the daughter of his dead business partner—Captain Crewe! "Do you suppose," he said, "that the other child could possibly be reduced to any such condition as the poor little soul next door?"

He had been trying to find Captain Crewe's daughter, a girl whose first name and whose school he did not know, so that he might give to her her father's half of the wealth finally received from the diamond mines. This was the trouble on his mind.

*   *   *

The winter was a wretched one. There were days on which Sara tramped through snow when she went on her errands; there were worse days when the snow melted into slush; there were others when the fog was so thick that the lamps in the street were lighted all day and London looked as it had looked the afternoon, several years ago, when the cab had driven through the streets with Sara tucked up on its seat, leaning against her father's shoulder.

For several days it had rained continuously; the streets were chilly and sloppy and full of dreary, cold mist; there was mud everywhere. Of course there were several long and tiresome errands to be done— there always were on days like this—and Sara was sent out again and again, until her shabby clothes were damp through. Added to this, she had been deprived of her dinner, because Miss Minchin had chosen to punish her. She was so cold and hungry and tired that her face began to have a pinched look, and now and then some kind-hearted person passing her in the street glanced at her with sympathy. The muddy water squelched through her broken shoes and the wind seemed to be trying to drag her thin jacket from her.

"Suppose I had dry clothes on," she thought. "Suppose I had good shoes and a long, thick coat and stockings and an umbrella. And suppose—suppose— just when I was near a baker's where they sold hot buns, I should find sixpence—which belonged to nobody. *Suppose*, if I did, I should go into the shop and buy six of the hottest buns and eat them all without stopping."

Some very odd things happen in this world sometimes.

It certainly was an odd thing that happened to Sara. She had to cross the street just when she was saying this to herself. The mud was dreadful. She had to look down at her feet and the mud, and in looking down—just as she reached the pavement—she saw something shining in the gutter. It was actually a piece of silver—a tiny piece trodden upon by many feet. Not quite a sixpence, but the next thing to it—a fourpenny piece.

In one second it was in her cold little red-and-blue hand.

"Oh," she gasped, "it is true! It is true!"

And then, if you will believe me, she looked straight at the shop directly facing her. And it was a baker's shop, and a cheerful, stout, motherly woman with rosy cheeks was putting into the window a tray of delicious newly baked hot buns, fresh from the oven— large, plump, shiny buns, with currants in them.

She crossed the pavement and put her wet foot on the step. As she did so she saw something that made her stop.

It was a little figure more forlorn even than herself— a little figure which was not much more than a bundle of rags, from which small, bare, red muddy feet peeped out, only because the rags with which their owner was trying to cover them were not long enough. Above the rags appeared a shock of tangled hair, and a dirty face with big, hollow, hungry eyes.

Sara knew they were hungry eyes. "She is hungrier than I am," she said to herself.

The child stared up at Sara.

Sara spoke to her. "Are you hungry?"

"Ain't I jist?" she said in a hoarse voice.

"Haven't you had any dinner?"

"No dinner, not yet no bre'fast—nor yet no supper. No nothin'."

"Since when?"

"Dunno. Never got nothin' today—nowhere. I've axed an' axed."

Sara said to herself, "Buns are a penny each. If it had been sixpence I could have eaten six. It won't be enough for either of us. But it will be better than nothing."

"Wait a minute," she said to the beggar child.

She went into the shop. It was warm and smelled deliciously. The woman was just going to put some more hot buns into the window.

"If you please," said Sara, "have you lost four-pence—a silver fourpence?"

The woman looked at it and then at her.

"Bless us, no," she answered. "Did you find it?"

"Yes," said Sara. "In the gutter."

"Keep it, then," said the woman. "It may have been there for a week, and goodness knows who lost it. Do you want to buy something?"

"Four buns, if you please," said Sara. "Those at a penny each."

The woman went to the window and put some in a paperbag.

Sara noticed she had put in six.

"I said four, if you please," she said. "I have only fourpence."

"I'll throw in two," said the woman. "I dare say you can eat them sometime. Aren't you hungry?"

"Yes," Sara answered. "I am very hungry, and I am much obliged to you for your kindness—" But just at that moment two or three customers came in at once, and each one seemed in a hurry, so she could only thank the woman again and go out.

The beggar girl was still huddled up in the corner of the step. She looked frightful in her wet and dirty rags.

Sara opened the paper bag and took out one of the hot buns.

"See," she said, putting the bun in the ragged lap, "this is nice and hot. Eat it, and you will not feel so hungry."

The girl snatched up the bun and began to cram it into her mouth with great wolfish bites. "Oh, my! Oh, my!" she said hoarsely, "Oh, my!"

Sara took out three more buns and put them down. "She is hungrier than I am," she said to herself. "She's starving. I'm not," she said, as she put down the fifth bun.

The little London savage was still snatching and devouring when Sara turned away.

"Good-bye," said Sara.

When she reached the other side of the street she looked back. The child had a bun in each hand and had stopped in the middle of a bite to watch her. Sara gave her a little nod, and the child jerked her shaggy head in response.

Sara found some comfort in her remaining bun. As she walked along she broke off small pieces and ate them slowly to make them last longer.

"Suppose it was a magic bun," she said, "and a bite was as much as a whole dinner. I should be overeating myself if I went on like this."

CHAPTER 7
The Queen's Table

WHEN SARA RETURNED to the house, Miss Minchin demanded, "Where have you wasted your time? You have been out for hours."

"It was so wet and muddy," Sara answered, "it was hard to walk."

Sara went into the cook. "Here are the things."

The cook looked them over, grumbling.

"May I have something to eat?" Sara asked.

"Tea's over and done with," was the answer. "Did you expect me to keep it hot for you?"

"I had no dinner," said Sara.

"There's some bread in the pantry," said the cook. "That's all you'll get at this time of day."

Sara went and found the bread. It was old and hard and dry.

Really, it was hard for the child to climb the three long flights of stairs leading to her attic. When she reached the top landing she was glad to see the glimmer of a light coming from under her door. That meant that Ermengarde had managed to creep up to pay her a visit.

Ermengarde was sitting in the middle of the bed. "Oh, Sara," she cried out, "You do look tired, Sara. You are quite pale."

"I *am* tired," said Sara. "Oh, there's Melchisedec, poor thing. He's come to ask for his supper."

The rat had come out of his hole as if he had been listening for her footstep. Sara was quite sure he knew it. He came forward as Sara put her hand in her pocket and turned it inside out.

"I'm very sorry," she said. "I haven't got one crumb left. Go home, Melchisedec, and tell your wife there was nothing in my pocket. I'm afraid I forgot because the cook and Miss Minchin were so cross."

The rat seemed to understand. He shuffled back to his home.

"I wish I was as thin as you, Sara," said Ermengarde. "I believe you are thinner than you used to be. Your eyes look so big, and the sharp little bones are sticking out of your elbow."

They both heard a sound that checked their conversation. It came from on the stairs below, and it was Miss Minchin's angry voice. Sara sprang off the bed and put out the candle.

"You rude, dishonest child!" they heard her say.

" 'T warn't me, mum," said Becky's voice, sobbing.

"Don't tell falsehoods," said Miss Minchin. "Go to your room this instant."

Both Sara and Ermengarde heard the slap, and then heard Becky run in her shoes up the stairs and into her attic.

Sara stood in the middle of the room in the darkness. She was clenching her little teeth and opening and shutting her hands.

"Miss Minchin is a wicked, cruel thing!" she burst forth. "The cook takes things herself and then says Becky steals them. She *doesn't!* She *doesn't!* She's so hungry sometimes that she eats crusts out of the ash barrel!" She pressed her hands against her face and burst into sobs. Ermengarde, hearing the unconquerable Sara crying, had a new possibility present itself to her kind, slow, little mind all at once. She struck a match and lit the candle. She bent forward and looked at Sara.

"Sara," she said, "are—are—you never told me—I don't want to be rude, but—are you ever hungry?"

Sara lifted her face from her hands. "Yes," she said. "Yes, I am. I'm so hungry now. And it makes it worse to hear poor Becky. She's hungrier than I am."

Ermengarde gasped. "Oh, oh!" she cried. "And I never knew!"

"I didn't want you to know," Sara said. "It would have made me feel like a street beggar. I know I look like a street beggar."

"No, you don't—you don't!" Ermengarde broke in. "Your clothes are a little strange—but you couldn't look like a street beggar.—Oh, Sara, this very afternoon my nicest aunt sent me a box. It's full of good things. I never touched it, I had so much pudding at dinner. It's got cake in it, and little meat pies, and jam tarts and buns, and oranges and figs and chocolate. I'll creep back to my room and get in this minute, and we'll eat it now."

"Do you think you *could?*" exclaimed Sara.

"I know I could," answered Ermengarde.

It was so delightful that they caught each other's hands and Sara said, "Ermie! Let us *pretend!* Let us pretend it's a party. And, oh, won't you invite the prisoner in the next cell?"

"Yes! Yes! Let us knock on the wall now. The jailer won't hear."

Almost immediately after the knocks, the door of the attic opened and Becky appeared. Her eyes were red.

"Miss Ermengarde has asked you to come in, Becky," said Sara, "because she is going to bring a box of good things up here to us."

"To eat, miss?" she said.

"Yes," answered Sara, "and we are going to pretend a party."

Ermengarde tiptoed out of the attic.

"Oh, miss!" said Becky now to Sara. "I know it was you that asked her to let me come. It—it makes me cry to think of it."

"Somehow, something always happens," said Sara, "just before the very worst. It is as if the Magic did it. If I could only just remember that always. The worst thing never *quite* comes.—We must make haste and set the table."

"Set the table, miss?" said Becky. "What'll we set it with?"

Within a few minutes Becky had her answer; Magic had transformed an old table covered with a red shawl and set with rubbish from a long-unopened trunk into a banquet hall.

Ermengarde came in soon after. "Oh, Sara," she cried out. "You are the cleverest girl I ever saw!"

"Isn't it nice?" said Sara. "They are things out of my old trunk. I asked my Magic, and it told me to go and look."

"It's like a real party!" cried Ermengarde.

"It's like a queen's table," sighed Becky.

"I'll tell you what, Sara," said Ermengarde. "Pretend you are a princess now and this is a royal feast."

"But it's your feast," said Sara. "You must be the princess and we will be your maids of honor."

"Oh, I can't," said Ermengarde. "I'm too fat, and I don't know how. *You* be her."

"Well, if you want me to," said Sara.

She led the way to the table. She waved her hand graciously to Ermengarde and Becky.

"Advance, fair damsels," she said in her happy dream-voice, "and be seated at the banquet table."

They had barely had time to take their pieces of cake into their hands when they all three sprang to their feet and turned faces toward the door—listening—listening.

Someone was coming up the stairs.

"It's the missus!" choked Becky, and dropped her piece of cake upon the floor.

"Yes," said Sara. "Miss Minchin has found us out."

Miss Minchin struck the door open with a blow of her hand. "I have been suspecting something of this sort," she exclaimed; "but I did not dream of such audacity. Lavinia was telling the truth."

Miss Minchin strode over to Becky and boxed her ears.

"You rude creature!" she said. "You leave the house in the morning!"

"Oh, don't send her away," sobbed Ermengarde. "My aunt sent me the hamper. We're—only—having a party."

"So I see," said Miss Minchin. "With the Princess Sara at the head of the table." She turned on Sara. "It is your doing, I know. Ermengarde would never have thought of such a thing. You decorated the table, I suppose—with this rubbish." She stamped her foot at Becky. "Go to your attic!" she commanded, and Becky stole away.

Then it was Sara's turn again.

"I will attend to you tomorrow. You shall have neither breakfast, dinner, nor supper!"

"I have not had either dinner or supper today, Miss Minchin," said Sara.

"Then all the better. You will have something to remember. Don't stand there. Put those things into the hamper again.—And you," she said to Ermengarde, "take it back to your room and go back to bed. You will stay there all day tomorrow, and I shall write to your papa. What would *he* say if he knew where you are tonight?"

"I was wondering," said Sara in a low voice, "what *my* papa would say if he knew where I am tonight."

"You rude, unmanageable child!" cried Miss Minchin. "How dare you!"

She shut the door behind herself and Ermengarde, and left Sara standing quite alone.

CHAPTER 8

The Magic

T HE DREAM WAS quite at an end. Emily was sitting with her back against the wall, staring very hard. Sara saw her, and went and picked her up. "There isn't any banquet left, Emily," said Sara. "And there isn't any princess. There is nothing left but the prisoners in the Bastille." And she sat down and hid her face.

What would have happened if she had not hidden it just then, and if she had chanced to look up at the skylight at the wrong moment, I do not know, because if she had glanced at the skylight she would certainly have been startled by what she would have seen. She would have seen the Indian servant from next door.

But she did not look up; she went to bed.

"I can't pretend anything else—while I am awake," she said. "If I go to sleep, perhaps a dream will come and pretend for me."

She did not know how long she slept. When she awakened it was rather suddenly. There was a sound which had called her back—a real sound—the click of the skylight as it fell in closing after a thin white figure which slipped through it and crouched down close by upon the slates of the roof—just near enough to see what happened in the attic, but not near enough to be seen.

At first she did not open her eyes. She felt too sleepy and—strangely enough—too warm and comfortable. She was so warm and comfortable, indeed, that she did not believe she was really awake.

"What a nice dream!" she murmured. "I feel quite warm. I—don't—want—to—wake—up."

Of course it was a dream. She felt as if warm, delightful bedclothes were heaped upon her. She could actually feel blankets. And there was a sense of light, and a sound—the sound of a crackling, roaring little fire.

"Oh, I am awakening," she said. "I can't help it—I can't."

Her eyes opened in spite of herself. "Oh, I haven't awakened," she whispered. "I am dreaming yet." She knew it *must* be a dream, for if she were awake such things could not be.

This is what she saw. In the grate there was a glowing, blazing fire; on the hob was a little brass kettle hissing and boiling; spread upon the floor was a thick, warm red rug; before the fire a chair, with cushions on it; by the chair a table, covered by a small cloth, and upon it spread small covered dishes, a cup, a saucer, a teapot; on the bed were new warm coverings and a satin-covered down quilt; at the foot a strange silk robe, a pair of slippers, and some books. The room of her dream seemed changed into

fairyland—and it was flooded with warm light, for a bright lamp stood on the table covered with a rosy shade.

She sat up, resting on her elbow, and her breathing came short and fast.

"It does not—melt away," she said. "Oh, I never had such a dream before."

The blazing fire drew her to it, and she knelt down and held out her hands close to it—so close that the heat made her start back.

"A fire I only dreamed wouldn't be *hot*," she cried.

She sprang up, touched the table, the dishes, the rug; she went to the bed and touched the blankets. She took up the soft dressing-gown, and suddenly clutched it to her chest and held it to her cheek.

"It's warm, it's soft!" she almost sobbed. "It's real. It must be!"

She threw it over her shoulders, and put her feet into the slippers.

"They are real, too. It's all real," she cried. "I am *not* dreaming."

She went to the books and opened the one which lay upon the top. Something was written upon the blank page at the start of the book—just a few words:

"To the little girl in the attic. From a friend."

When she saw that, she burst into tears.

"I don't know who it is," she said; "but somebody cares for me a little. I have a friend."

She took her candle and stole out of her own room and into Becky's, and stood by her bedside.

"Becky!" she whispered. "Wake up!"

When Becky wakened, her face still smudged with traces of tears, beside her stood a little figure in a luxurious robe of red silk. The face she saw was a shining, wonderful thing. The Princess Sara stood at her very bedside, holding a candle in her hand.

"Come," she said. "Oh, Becky, come!"

Becky got up and followed her.

When they crossed the threshold, Sara shut the door and drew her into the warm, glowing midst of things.

"It's true! It's true!" she cried. "I've touched them all and they are as real as we are. The Magic has come and done it, Becky, while we were asleep—the Magic that won't let those worst things *ever* quite happen."

Imagine, if you can, what the rest of the evening was like. How they crouched by the fire. How they removed the covers of the dishes, and found rich, hot, tasty soup, and sandwiches and muffins enough for both of them. The tea was so delicious that it was not necessary to pretend that it was anything but tea. Sara had lived such a life of imaginings that she was quite equal to accepting any wonderful thing that happened.

The sleepy comfort which overpowered the girls was a heavenly thing. There were even blankets enough to share with Becky. As she went out of the room, Becky turned upon the threshold and said, "If it ain't here in the mornin', miss, it's been here tonight, anyways, an' I shan't never forget it."

It was quite well known in the morning, throughout the school, that Sara Crewe was in horrible disgrace, that Ermengarde was under punishment, and Becky would have been packed out of the house before breakfast, but that a scullery maid, helpless and humble enough to work like a slave, could not be found.

If it was possible for weather to be worse than it had been the day before, it was worse this day—wetter, muddier, colder. There were more errands to be done. But what does anything matter when one's Magic has just proved itself one's friend. Sara's supper of the night before had given her strength, she knew that she should sleep well and warmly, and, even though she had begun to be hungry again before evening, she felt that she could bear it until breakfast on the following day, when her meals would surely be given to her again. It was quite late when she was allowed to go upstairs.

She pushed the attic door open and went in. She gasped. The Magic had been there again. The fire was blazing. A number of new things had been brought into the attic. Under the low table another supper stood—this time with cups and plates for Becky as well as herself. All the bare ugly things which could be covered with draperies had been concealed and made to look quite pretty.

Sara sat down and looked again and again.

"It is exactly like something fairy come true. I feel as if I might wish for anything—diamonds or bags of gold—and they would appear! The one thing I always wanted was to see a fairy story come true. I am *living* in a fairy story."

She rose and knocked upon the wall for the prisoner in the next cell, and the prisoner came.

When Becky entered she gasped, "Oh, laws, miss!"

On this night Becky sat on a cushion upon the hearth rug and had a cup and saucer of her own.

When Sara went to bed she found that she had a new thick mattress and big downy pillows.

"Where does it all come from?" asked Becky.

"Don't let us even *ask*," said Sara. "If it were not that I want to say, 'Oh, thank you,' I would rather not know. It makes it more beautiful."

From that time life became more wonderful day by day. The fairy story continued. Almost every day something new was done. In a short time the attic was a beautiful little room full of all sorts of odd and luxurious things. When Sara went downstairs in the morning, the remains of the supper were on the table; and when she returned to the attic in the evening, the magician had removed them and left another nice little meal. Miss Minchin, however, was as harsh and insulting as ever. Sara was sent on errands in all weathers, and scolded and driven hither and thither; she was scarcely allowed to talk to Ermengarde; Lavinia sneered at the increasing shabbiness of her clothes; and the other girls stared at her when she appeared in the schoolroom. But what did it matter while she was living in this wonderful story?

In a very short time she began to look less thin. Color came into her cheeks, and her eyes did not seem so much too big for her face. Very naturally, even Becky was beginning to look plumper and less frightened. The Bastille had melted away, the prisoners no longer existed.

"I can't help thinking about my friend," said Sara to Becky. "If he wants to keep himself a secret, it would be rude to try and find out who he is. But I do so want him to know how thankful I am to him—and how happy he has made me.—Oh, I can write to him! And leave it on the table. Then perhaps the person who takes the things away will take it, too."

So she wrote a note:

I hope you will not think it is impolite that I should write this note to you when you wish to keep yourself a secret. Please believe I only want to thank you for being so kind to me and making everything like a fairy story. I am so grateful to you, and I am so happy—and so is Becky. We used to be so lonely and cold and hungry, and now—oh, just think what you have done for us! Thank *you*—thank *you*—thank *you*!

                    THE LITTLE GIRL IN THE ATTIC.

CHAPTER 9

"It Is the Child"

THE NEXT MORNING she left this on the little table, and in the evening it had been taken away with the other things; so she knew the Magician had received it, and she was happier for the thought.

She was reading one of her new books to Becky just before they went to bed, when her attention was attracted by a sound at the skylight.

"It sounds rather like a cat trying to get in," said Sara.

She climbed on a chair, raised the skylight, and peeped out. It had been snowing all day, and on the snow crouched a tiny, shivering figure, whose small black face wrinkled itself.

"It is the monkey," she cried out. "He has crept out of the Indian servant's attic."

"Are you going to let him in, miss?'"

"Yes," Sara answered. "It's too cold for monkeys to be out."

She put a hand out. "Come along, monkey darling. I won't hurt you."

He let her lift him through the skylight, and when he found himself in her arms he cuddled up to her breast and looked up into her face.

"Nice monkey, nice monkey!" she crooned, kissing his funny head. "Oh, I do love little animals."

"What shall you do with him?" Becky asked.

"I shall let him sleep with me tonight, and then take him back to the Indian gentleman tomorrow."

And when she went to bed she made him a nest at her feet, and he curled up and slept there as if he were a baby.

In the morning, Ram Dass, the Indian servant, went to Mr. Carrisford's room to announce: "Sahib, the child has come—the child the sahib felt pity for. She brings back the monkey who had again run away to her attic under the roof. I have asked that she remain. It was my thought that it would please the sahib to see and speak with her."

"Yes, I should like to see her. Go and bring her in." Ram Dass had told Mr. Carrisford of the child's miseries, and together they had invented their romantic plan to help her by bringing her food, books and furniture.

Then Sara came into the room. She carried the monkey in her arms. "Your monkey ran away again," she said. "He came to my attic window last night, and I took him in because it was so cold. I would have brought him back if it had not been so late. I knew you were ill and might not like to be disturbed."

"That was very thoughtful of you," said the Indian gentleman.

Sara looked toward Ram Dass, who stood near the door.

"Shall I give him to the Lascar?" she asked.

"How do you know Ram Dass is a Lascar?" said the Indian gentleman.

"Oh, I know Lascars," Sara said. "I was born in India."

The Indian gentleman sat upright suddenly. "You were born in India!" he exclaimed. "Where is your papa?"

"He died," said Sara, very quietly. "He lost all his money and there was none left for me. There was no one to take care of me or to pay Miss Minchin."

"So you were sent up into the attic, and made into a little drudge.—How did your father lose his money?"

"He did not lose it himself. He had a friend he was very fond of. It was his friend who took the money. He trusted his friend too much."

The Indian gentleman's breath came quickly. "The friend might have meant to do no harm. It might have happened through a mistake."

"The suffering was just as bad for my papa," said Sara. "It killed him."

"What was your father's name?" the Indian gentleman said. "Tell me."

"His name was Ralph Crewe. Captain Crewe. He died in India."

"It is the child—the child!"

"What child am I?"

"I am your father's friend. We have been looking for you for two years."

Sara spoke as if she were in a dream. "And I was at Miss Minchin's all the while. Just on the other side of the wall."

The excitement of the totally unexpected discovery almost overpowered Mr. Carrisford in his weak condition.

His friends, the members of the Large Family, came over to take care of Sara.

Their real name was Carmichael. Mrs. Carmichael took Sara in her arms and kissed her.

"You look bewildered, poor child," she said.

"Was he," asked Sara, "was *he* the wicked friend?"

Mrs. Carmichael was crying as she kissed Sara again. "He was not wicked, my dear. He did not really lose your papa's money. He only thought he had lost it; and because he loved him so much his grief made him so ill that for a time he was not in his right mind. He almost died of brain fever, and long before he began to recover your poor papa was dead."

"And he did not know where to find me," murmured Sara. "And I was so near."

"He believed you were in school in France," explained Mrs. Carmichael. "He has looked for you everywhere. When he saw you pass by, looking so sad and neglected, he did not dream that you were his friend's poor child. But because you were a little girl, too, he was sorry for you, and wanted to make you happier. And he told Ram Dass to climb into your attic window and try to make you comfortable."

Sara gave a start of joy. "Did Ram Dass bring the things?" she cried out. "Did he tell Ram Dass to do it? Did he make that dream come true?"

"Yes, my dear—yes! He is kind and good, and he was sorry for you, for little lost Sara Crewe's sake."

She went and appeared before Mr. Carrisford. "You sent the things to me," she said. "The beautiful things!"

"Yes, poor child, I did," he answered her.

"Then it is you who are my friend," she said. And she took his hand and kissed it again and again.

The plan now was that Sara was not to return to the school at all. Mr. Carrisford was very determined she must remain where she was, and Mr. Carmichael should go and see Miss Minchin about it.

"I am glad I need not go back," said Sara. "She will be very angry. She does not like me; though perhaps it is my fault, because I do not like her."

But, oddly enough, Miss Minchin made it unnecessary for Mr. Carmichael to go to her, by actually coming in search of her pupil herself.

Sara was sitting on a footstool close to Mr. Carrisford's knee, and listening to some of the many things he felt it necessary to try to explain to her, when Ram Dass announced the visitor's arrival.

Miss Minchin entered the room. "I am sorry to disturb Mr. Carrisford," she said. "I am Miss Minchin, the owner of the Young Ladies' Seminary next door."

"So, you are Miss Minchin," said the Indian gentleman.

"I am, sir. I have come here as a matter of duty. I have just discovered that you have been intruded upon through the forwardness of one of my pupils—a charity pupil. I came to explain that she intruded without my knowledge." She turned upon Sara. "Go home at once! You shall be severely punished. Go home."

The Indian gentleman drew Sara to his side and patted her hand. "She is not going."

"Not going!" said Miss Minchin.

"No," said Mr. Carrisford. "She is not going *home*—if you give your house that name. Her home for the future will be with me."

"With *you!* With *you,* sir!"

Then Mr. Carmichael explained: "Mr. Carrisford, madam, was a close friend of the late Captain Crewe. He was his partner in certain large investments. The fortune which Captain Crewe supposed he had lost has been recovered, and is now in Mr. Carrisford's hands."

"The fortune!" cried Miss Minchin. "Sara's fortune!"

"It is Sara's fortune now, in fact," said Mr. Carmichael. "The diamond mines have increased it enormously."

"The diamond mines!"

"There are not many princesses," said Mr. Carmichael, "who are richer than your little charity pupil, Sara Crewe, will be. Mr. Carrisford has been searching for her for nearly two years; he has found her at last, and he will keep her."

"He found her under my care," Miss Minchin protested. "I have done everything for her. But for me she should have starved in the streets."

"As to starving in the streets," called out Mr. Carrisford, who was angered by her statement, "she might have starved more comfortably there than in your attic."

"She must finish her education!" argued Miss Minchin. "The law will interfere in my behalf."

"Come, come," interrupted the lawyer Mr. Carmichael. "The law will do nothing of the sort. If Sara herself wishes to return to you, I dare say Mr. Carrisford might not refuse to allow it. But that rests with Sara."

"Then," said Miss Minchin, "I appeal to Sara. I have not spoiled you, perhaps, but you know I have always been fond of you."

Sara's eyes fixed themselves on Miss Minchin. "Have you, Miss Minchin? I did not know that."

"You ought to have known it," said Miss Minchin. "Will you not do your duty to your poor papa and come home with me?"

Sara was thinking of the day when she had been told that she belonged to nobody, and was in danger of being turned out into the street; she was thinking of the cold, hungry hours she had spent alone with Emily and Melchisedec in the attic. She looked Miss Minchin in the face.

"You know why I will not go home with you, Miss Minchin," she said; "you know quite well."

A hot flush showed itself on Miss Minchin's hard, angry face. She said to the Indian gentleman, as she turned to leave the room, "You have not undertaken an easy charge. You will discover that very soon. The child is neither truthful nor grateful. I suppose"—to Sara—"that you feel now that you are a princess again."

"I tried not to be anything else," she answered. "Even when I was coldest and hungriest—I tried not to be."

"Now it will not be necessary to try," said Miss Minchin, as Ram Dass salaamed her out of the room.

That evening, when the pupils were gathered together before the fire in the schoolroom, Ermengarde came in with a letter in her hand and an odd expression on her round face.

"What is the matter?" cried two or three voices at once.

"I have just had this letter from Sara," she said, holding it out to let them see what a long letter it was.

"From Sara! Where is she?"

"Next door," said Ermengarde, "with the Indian gentleman."

"Where? Where? Why? Tell us! Tell us!"

Ermengarde answered them slowly. "There *were* diamond mines; there *were!*"

Almost until midnight the entire school crowded round Ermengarde in the schoolroom and heard read and re-read the letter containing a story which was quite as wonderful as any Sara had ever invented.

Becky, who had heard it also, managed to creep upstairs earlier than usual. She wanted to get away from people and go and look at the magic little room once more. Glad as she was for Sara's sake, she went up the last flight of stairs with tears blurring her sight. There would be no fire tonight, and no rosy lamp; no supper, and no princess sitting in the glow reading or telling stories—no princess!

She choked down a sob as she pushed the attic door open.

The lamp was flushing the room, the fire was blazing, the supper was waiting; and Ram Dass was standing smiling.

"Missee sahib remembered," he said. "She told the sahib all. She wished you to know the good fortune which has befallen her. Behold a letter on the tray. She has written. She did not wish that you should go to sleep unhappy. The sahib commands you to come to him tomorrow. You are to be the attendant of missee sahib."

And having said this, he made a little salaam and slipped through the skylight.

CHAPTER 10

Anne

IN A MONTH'S time, Mr. Carrisford was a new man.
There were so many charming things to plan for
Sara. There was a little joke between them that he
was a magician, and it was one of his pleasures to
invent things to surprise her. She found beautiful new
flowers growing in her room, little gifts under pillows,
and once, as they sat together in the evening, they
heard the scratch of a heavy paw on the door, and
when Sara went to find out what it was, there stood a
great dog with a grand silver and gold collar bearing
an inscription: "I am Boris. I serve the Princess Sara."

One evening, Mr. Carrisford, looking up from his book, noticed that his companion sat gazing into the fire.

"What are you 'supposing,' Sara?"

"I was remembering that hungry day, and a child I saw." She told him the story of the bun shop, and the fourpence she picked up out of the sloppy mud, and the child who was hungrier than herself. "And I was supposing a kind of plan. I was thinking I should like to do something. You say I have so much money—I was wondering if I could go to see the bun-woman, and tell her that if, when hungry children—particularly on those dreadful days—come and sit on the steps, or look in the window, she would just call them in and give them something to eat, she might send the bills to me. Could I do that?"

"You shall do it tomorrow morning," said the Indian gentleman.

"Thank you," said Sara. "You see, I know what it is to be hungry, and it is very hard when one cannot even *pretend* it away."

The next morning, Sara, accompanied by Mr. Carrisford, rode a carriage to the door of the baker's shop.

When Sara entered the shop, the bun-woman turned and looked at her, and, leaving the buns, came and stood behind the counter. For a moment she looked at Sara very hard indeed, and then her good-natured face lighted up.

"I'm sure that I remember you," she said. "And yet—"

"Yes," said Sara; "once you gave me six buns for fourpence, and ——"

"And you gave five of 'em to a beggar child," the woman broke in on her. "I've always remembered it. Excuse the liberty, miss, but you look rosier and better than you did that time."

"I am better, thank you," said Sara. "And I am much happier—and I have come to ask you to do something for me."

"Me, miss!" exclaimed the bun-woman. "What can I do?"

And then Sara, leaning on the counter, made her little proposal concerning the dreadful days and the hungry children and the buns.

"Why, bless me!" she said. "It'll be a pleasure to do it. I am a working-woman myself and cannot afford to do much, but I'm bound to say I've given away many a bit of bread since that afternoon, just along o' thinking of you—an' how wet an' cold you was, an' how hungry you looked; an' yet you gave away your hot buns as if you was a princess."

"She looked so hungry," said Sara. "She was even hungrier than I was."

"She was starving," said the woman. "Many's the time she's told me of it since—how she sat there in the wet, and felt as if a wolf was a-tearing at her poor young insides."

"Oh, have you seen her since then? Do you know where she is?"

"Yes, I do," said the woman. "Why, she's in that

there back room, miss, an' has been for a month; an' a decent, well-meanin' girl she's goin' to turn out, an' such a help to me in the shop an' in the kitchen as you'd scarce believe, knowin' how she's lived."

She stepped to the door of the little back parlor and spoke; and the next minute a girl came out and followed her behind the counter. And actually it was the beggar-child, clean and neatly clothed, and looking as if she had not been hungry for a long time. She knew Sara in an instant.

"You see," said the woman. "I told her to come when she was hungry, and when she'd come I'd give her odd jobs to do; an' I found she was willing, and somehow I got to like her; and the end of it was, I've given her a place an' a home, and she helps me, an' behaves well, an' is as thankful as a girl can be. Her name's Anne."

The children stood and looked at each other for a few moments; and then Sara held out her hand across the counter, and Anne took it.

"I am so glad," Sara said. "Perhaps Mrs. Brown will let you be the one to give the buns and bread to the children. Perhaps you would like to do it because you know what it is to be hungry, too."

"Yes, miss," said the girl.

And, somehow, Sara felt as if she understood her, though she said so little, and only stood still and looked after her as she went out of the shop with the Indian gentleman, and they got into the carriage and drove away.